SCOUT
and ACE

Flying in a Frying Pan

Written by Rose Impey
Illustrated by Ant Parker

Once upon a time, our heroes,

and

set out on a trip

into outer, outer-space.

Sucked through a worm-hole . . .

to a strange, new place,

ost in a galaxy called Fairy Tale Space.

"Uh, oh. Look out," says Scout.
"That's one scary face," says Ace.

It's a space-witch with
a mean-looking cat.
And she's flying in a frying pan!

Ace pulls a face and the witch's cat pulls one back.

Now the witch has seen them.

"Look what you've done, you crazy cat!" shouts Scout.

"Come on!" squeals Ace.
"It's a race!"

Boom! **Boom!** ZOOM!

Scout and Ace zoom away.
And the witch zooms after them.

The witch has three tricks
up her sleeve.
First she throws her magic
hairnet after them.

The hairnet grows bigger...

and bigger..

until . . .

... it catches the spaceship.

But the SuperStar snips
its way out.

Next the witch throws her
magic comb after them.

The comb grows bigger . . .

and bigger . . .

until . . .

... it blocks the spaceship's path.

"Yes!" squeals the witch.

But the SuperStar saws
its way out.

Next the witch throws her magic teeth after them.

The teeth come closer . . .

and closer . .

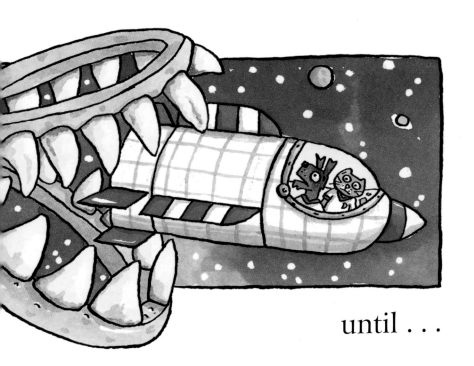

until . . .

. . . they snap like a trap. "Yes!" squeals the witch. "Let's take those teeth out," shouts Scout.

"Kapow!" says Ace. "Take that."

"Ow! Ow! Ow!" cries the witch and her mean-looking cat.

The SuperStar zooms away.

And Scout and Ace live
to fight another day.

"Great race," says Ace.
But Scout looks cross.
"Keep your hairnet on, Captain,"
Ace tells him.

"No need to fly off the handle.
Broom! Broom!"
Scout groans. "Let's get out
of here," he moans.

Fire the engines...

and lower the dome.

Once more our heroes...

are heading for home.

Enjoy all these stories about

SCOUT and ACE

and their adventures in Spa

Scout and Ace: Kippers for Supper
1 84362 172 X

Scout and Ace: Flying in a Frying Pan
1 84362 171 1

Scout and Ace: Stuck on Planet Gloo
1 84362 173 8

Scout and Ace: Kissing Frogs
1 84362 176 2

Scout and Ace: Talking Tables
1 84362 174 6

Scout and Ace: A Cat, a Rat and a Bat
1 84362 175 4

Scout and Ace: Three Heads to Feed
1 84362 177 0

Scout and Ace: The Scary Bear
1 84362 178 9

All priced at £4.99 each.

Colour Crunchies are available from all good bookshops, or can be ordered direct from the publ
Orchard Books, PO BOX 29, Douglas MM99 1BQ.
Credit card orders please telephone 01624 836000 or fax 01624 837033
or email: bookshop@enterprise.net for details.

To order please quote title, author and ISBN and your full name and address. Cheques and pos
orders should be made payable to 'Bookpost plc'. Postage and packing is FREE within the UI
overseas customers should add £1.00 per book. Prices and availability are subject to change

ORCHARD BOOKS, 96 Leonard Street, London EC2A 4XD.
Orchard Books Australia, 32/45-51 Huntley Street, Alexandria, NSW 2015.
This edition first published in Great Britain in hardback in 2004. First paperback publication 2005.
Text © Rose Impey 2004. Illustrations © Ant Parker 2004. The rights of Rose Impey to be identified as
the author and Ant Parker to be identified as the illustrator have been asserted by them in accordance with the
Copyright, Designs and Patents Act, 1988. A CIP catalogue record for this book is available from the British Library.
ISBN 1 84362 171 1   10 9 8 7 6 5 4 3 2
Printed in China